making
a
friend

making a friend

by Alison McGhee
with illustrations by Marc Rosenthal

Atheneum Books for Young Readers
New York London Toronto Sydney

Atheneum Books for Young Readers

An imprint of Simon & Schuster Children's Publishing Division

1230 Avenue of the Americas, New York, New York 10020

For information about special discounts for bulk purchases, please contact Simon & Schuster Special Sales at 1-866-506-1949 or business@simonandschuster.com.

The Simon & Schuster Speakers Bureau can bring authors to your live event. For more information or to book an event, contact the Simon & Schuster Speakers Bureau at 1-866-248-3049 or visit our website at www.simonspeakers.com.

Book design by Ann Bobco

The text for this book is set in Adobe Jenson.

The illustrations for this book are rendered in pencil and then manipulated digitally.

Manufactured in China

0711 SCP

First Edition

10 9 8 7 6 5 4 3 2 1

Library of Congress Cataloging-in-Publication Data

McGhee, Alison, 1960–

Making a friend / Alison McGhee ; illustrated by Marc Rosenthal. — 1st ed.

p.   cm.

Summary: When the snow falls, a young boy makes a snowman that becomes his friend until the seasons change.

ISBN 978-1-4169-8998-1

[1. Snow—Fiction. 2. Snowmen—Fiction. 3. Friendship—Fiction. 4. Seasons—Fiction.]

I. Rosenthal, Marc, 1949– ill. II. Title.

PZ7.M4784675Mak 2011

[E]—dc22   2010041661

To Caitlyn, with love
—A. M.

To Caitlyn Dlouhy and Holly McGhee, for pushing me
out of my comfort zone
—M. R.

Look.

The leaves are turning.

The air is growing cold.

Dream of winter.

On a moonless night, starry snow drifts down.

Wake to whiteness.

Snow.

Cold clean snow.

Sparkling snow.

Snow on your tongue.

Angels in the snow.

And a snowman.

You need a mouth, Snowman.

And a nose and eyes.

And arms.

And a hat.

I'll give you mine.

Snowman.

My snowman.

Snowman,
you left your hat.

Where did you go?

Where did he go?

Look.

He is in the falling water,

and the rain upon the ocean.

What you love will always be with you.

But where is he now?

He is there in the fog in the hollow,

and the frost on the window.

The leaves are turning again.

What you love

will always be with you.

Will he ever come back?

Look.

The lake's first ice.

The air is growing cold.

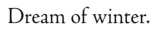

Dream of winter.

The first snow.

What you love...

will always be with you.

Snowman.

My snowman.